Bella's Saratoga Summer

Jennifer Gordon Sattler

Nicholas K. Burns Publishing
Utica, New York

Nicholas K. Burns Publishing
130 Proctor Boulevard
Utica, NY 13501

ISBN 0-9713069-3-1

Library of Congress Cataloging-in-Publication Data
Sattler, Jennifer Gordon.
Bella's Saratoga summer / Jennifer Gordon Sattler.
        p. cm.
Summary: Bella the elephant visits sites in Saratoga, New York, with her friend
Lily Duck, ending with a ride on Mayzie the racehorse.
        ISBN 0-9713069-3-1 (pbk.) — ISBN 0-9713069-4-X
[1. Elephants—Fiction. 2. Ducks—Fiction. 3. Saratoga (N.Y.)—Fiction.] I.
Title.
  PZ7.S24935 Be 2002
  [E]—dc21

                                                    2002004850

Printed & Bound in Hong Kong, China
by Book Art Inc., Toronto

For my funny, sweet, joyful girls, Mayzie and Lilia
and for Paul, who I love more than ice cream and pretzels.

Bella the elephant was hot and bored when a letter arrived

from her friend Lily Duck in Saratoga Springs, New York.

"Dearest Bella," it said, "Everything is nice and green here,

but I'm blue without you! Why don't you come for a visit?"

"Beep, beep!

I'm on my way to see my friend Lily Duck!" said Bella.

Bella's excitement made everyone on the bus giggle.

When she arrived in Saratoga Springs, Lily gave

Bella a big, downy hug and a wet ducky kiss.

Bella laughed when Lily's feathers tickled her long nose.

"You must be hungry, Bella," said Lily.

"Would you like some ice cream?"

"Moo!" said Bella.

"Moo!" laughed Lily as they licked their cones in a swing that looked like a cow.

"OOooee!! Ice cream sure makes me thirsty!" said Bella with a slurp.

"Let's get a drink," said Lily.

Lily warned Bella that the mineral water from the springs tasted kind of yucky...

But it makes you light as a bubble in the bathtub!

"Ploop, plip," said Bella the Bubble.

After their bath at the spa, the two friends

rowed a canoe on Saratoga Lake.

"Oh my, this is just lovely," Lily sighed.

"Ahoy, matey!" said Bella.

Later, Lily introduced Bella to her neighbors in Congress Park.

"This is Spit and that is Spat," she pointed to the fountain.

"Nice to meet you! You can call me...Squirt!" said Bella gracefully.

They blew wet kisses to their fountain friends and trotted off to Lily's favorite place, the Farmer's Market. The broccoli looked like tiny, tasty trees. Bella thought the cupcakes looked like pink petunia petals. The big, beautiful bananas were a real bargain. Lily bought lots and lots of those.

As they ate their picnic lunch,

Bella swayed to the music at SPAC.

"I'm having such a wonderful time, Lily," she whispered.

"Me too, Bella," said Lily, and she passed her friend another cupcake.

"Humm dee doodle doo!"

Bella was singing along to the music

that was still ringing through her great

big ears as she painted a picture of Lily

surrounded by the flowers at Yaddo.

"This is going on my refrigerator when I get home!" she said.

"When can we see the horses, Lily?" Bella asked, a bit impatiently.

"Soon Bella, but first you need a special hat."

They saw lots of great hats, but one hat made Bella clap her hands and squeal with delight. It had purple polka dots.

"That's it! It's *bee-u-ti-ful* !"

When the two buddies arrived at the race track,

Bella had to hug herself tightly because she was so excited.

"Look at that horse over there, Lily, she's wearing a hat like mine!"

They ran to meet the horse with the purple polka dots. "How do you do? My racing name is Marvelous Mayzie May," she said proudly, "but you may call me Mayzie. Your hat is simply *dee-light-ful* ! Would you care to join me for a ride?" asked the horse.

Bella climbed on Mayzie and they were off!

She felt like a bird as her ears flapped in the wind.

Speeding along the track she could hear everyone shouting,

"Go! Go! Go!"

Lily Duck was cheering loudest of all,

"Giddy-up, Mayzie! Yee haa, Bella!"

Bella was thanking Mayzie for the wild ride when Lily

quickly waddled up and gave her a big hug.

"Bella, this has been the best summer ever!" she said.

"It sure has Lily ol'pal, and do you know what my

favorite part was?"

"What?" asked Lily.

"Being with you!" said Bella. She gave Lily a big squeeze

and she laughed when Lily's feathers tickled her long nose.